Peter Piper and Pickles Peppers

Characters

Narrator

Peter Piper

Green Pepper

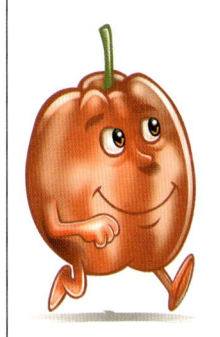
Red Pepper

Yellow Pepper

Setting

The Peter Piper Pepper Farm

Picture Words

Sight Words

am	I	in	like
me	that	will	you

peppers

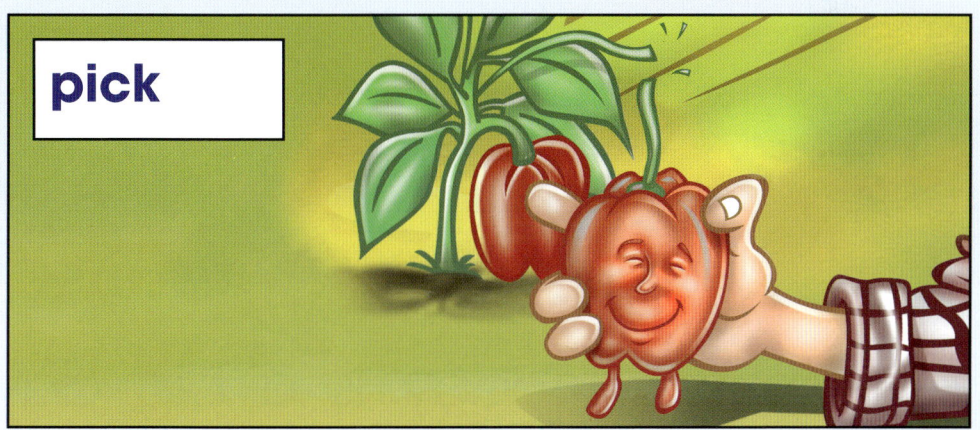

pick

Enrichment Words

gallons

peck

pickle

piper

Narrator: Today is a big day at the Peter Piper Pepper Farm. Today is pepper-picking day.

Peter Piper: I like peppers! I like to pick peppers.

Green Pepper: Pick me.
I am a green pepper.

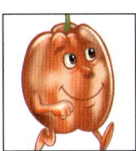
Red Pepper: Pick me.
I am a red pepper.

Yellow Pepper: Pick me.
I am a yellow pepper.

Peter Piper Pepper Farm

Pickled Peppers our Specialty

 **Peter:** You are pretty peppers. I will pick you, Green.

 **Green Pepper:** Ow!

 **Peter:** I will pick you, Red.

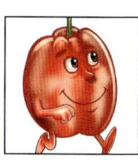
Red Pepper: Ow!

Yellow Pepper: What about me?

Peter: I will pick you too, Yellow.

Yellow Pepper: Ow!

 **Narrator:** Peter Piper picked a lot of peppers. He picked a peck of peppers.

 **Green Pepper:** A what?

 **Narrator:** A peck. A peck is the size of two gallons.

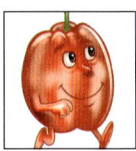 **Red Pepper:** That is a lot of peppers.

 **Yellow Pepper:** That is many, many peppers.

One Gallon + One Gallon = One Peck

 **Narrator:** Peter Piper liked to pickle peppers as much as he liked to pick peppers.

 **Peter:** I like to pickle peppers!

 **Narrator:** Peter Piper put peppers into a pot of pickle juice.

 **Peter:** Into the pot you go.

 **Green Pepper:** Yay! I will run in.

 **Red Pepper:** Yay! I will jump in.

 **Yellow Pepper:** Yay! I will dive in.

The End